A PRIVATE MATTER

A PRIVATE MATTER

by KATHRYN EWING

Illustrated by Joan Sandin

Scholastic Book Services
New York   Toronto   London   Auckland   Sydney

Text copyright © 1975 by Kathryn Ewing. Illustrations copyright © 1975 by Harcourt, Brace, Jovanovich, Inc. This edition is published by Scholastic Book Services, a division of Scholastic Magazines, Inc., by arrangement with Harcourt, Brace, Jovanovich, Inc.

12 11 10 9 8 7 6 5 4 3 2 1   11   6 7 8 9/7 0 1/8

Printed in the U.S.A.

To Douglas

Chapter 1

All afternoon after she got home from school and changed her clothes and ate the chocolate cupcake her mother had left for her in the refrigerator...all afternoon, Marcy sat on the front steps of her house and watched the people moving into 11 Morris Avenue next door.

Her first hopes had been dashed. She had hoped a family with children had bought the property. Even though her mother, who had sold the house for Barton Realty, had told her that

Mr. and Mrs. Charles Endicott had no children, still Marcy had kept hoping. Just because her mother had sold the house didn't mean she knew absolutely everything about the new owners. Back home in New Jersey where her mother said the Endicotts came from, there just might be a child or two; there might even be a nine-year-old girl, and that would be perfect for Marcy, the best thing that could happen in the whole world.

But it was obvious from the kind of stuff being unloaded from the big van that her mother had been right. No bicycles, no doll carriages, not even a play pen. Absolutely no children, boy or girl; no children of any kind whatever. It was equally obvious that Mr. and Mrs. Endicott were too old for children. At least, Mr. Endicott was. Marcy had seen Mrs. Endicott only once when she came down to the van, looked inside, threw up her hands, and ran back into the house again. Marcy had not gotten a good look at her except that she was little and fat.

Mr. Endicott, however, frequently came out of the house and went down to the van, walking up into it on the wooden ramp from the sidewalk. Sometimes he helped carry things, a lamp or a mirror, which Marcy thought was nice of him because the moving men all seemed so old and thin.

Every now and then he would look over to where Marcy sat on the porch steps and sometimes he'd toss her a wink or a grin. And right at the beginning when she came out to sit on the steps, he had called out, "Hi, Marcy. I'm Charles Endicott."

Naturally her mother had told him that her daughter's name was Marcy. She was surprised and pleased, however, that Mr. Endicott remembered it, although in response she had raised her hand only in a shy half wave. She liked Mr. Endicott. She liked the way he winked and the way his voice was crackly and deep.

Seated at the kitchen counter where they ate supper each night, Marcy told her mother about the furniture the Endicotts had: a green sofa, two gold chairs, a piano, and a lot of beds.

"I can't imagine what they will do with a lot of beds," her mother said, slicing her broiled chicken. "They have only two bedrooms."

"Twin beds for two bedrooms. That's four beds."

"Yes, that's a lot of beds," her mother answered, and then, beside her, the telephone rang.

Being in real estate, her mother got a lot of telephone calls. Frequently, as tonight, her mother's whole supper got cold while she talked to someone about mortgages or interest rates or leases. Her mother said she didn't mind the cold meal if it meant a sale, but she did feel bad because of Marcy and having no table conversation.

Marcy told her not to feel bad. She rather liked it that she didn't have to talk and could just eat.

And she could tell her mother enjoyed talking on the telephone about important things like real estate, and feeling alive and vital. Her mother was always telling Aunt Peg that real estate was her salvation because of being alive and vital. Marcy didn't see how anyone who wasn't dead could help feeling alive, but it was a big point with her mother.

Now Marcy slipped off her stool and went to a kitchen window. From this window she could look right down into the Endicotts' kitchen. Especially tonight, when there were no curtains up yet, she could get a superior view. Old Mrs. Geitner and her sister, who had lived in the house before, always snapped down their shades at night. She knew Mrs. Geitner and her sister were afraid of burglars. They kept double bolts on the doors, too. Marcy understood, but the house didn't look friendly.

The Endicotts' kitchen, on the other hand, even with boxes all piled around and everything, looked cozy and nice. The Endicotts sat at a table. She could see only Mrs. Endicott's hands now and then, pouring coffee or raising her water glass. But she could see almost all of Mr. Endicott. She watched him take a pipe from his jacket pocket and carefully insert it into a tobacco pouch. He put the pipe in his mouth and then took a pack of matches from the pocket on the other side of his jacket, struck one, and held the flame to the pipe bowl. After this he tilted his chair back on its hind legs, nice and comfortable. Then he happened to glance out his kitchen window, saw Marcy, and waved. Marcy waved back.

"Marcy!" her mother cried, interrupting her telephone conversation. "Marcy, come away from that window!"

Marcy spun around, but not before waving Mr. Endicott good-bye.

"You mustn't do that again, Marcy," her mother said after she had hung up and returned to her cold chicken.

"I wasn't doing anything," Marcy protested.

"Yes, you were. People don't look in other people's windows. It's not right."

"Mr. Endicott waved to me. He's nice."

"Yes. I think so, too. It's pleasant to have nice neighbors, but it won't be pleasant for them if you make them feel spied upon and uncomfortable."

"Mr. Endicott didn't mind."

"Marcy, it's not right. How about some chocolate ice cream for dessert?"

Marcy opened the freezer compartment and

took out the carton of ice cream. "Mr. Endicott smokes a pipe," she said. She didn't feel like telling her mother that she had just decided to marry a man who smoked a pipe. She also didn't feel like telling her mother about a plan that had begun to form in her mind.

The next day she hurried home after school and quickly changed her clothes. Then she went to the refrigerator and took out the cup of custard her mother had left for her on the treat shelf. Keeping well back from the window, she dipped her spoon into the dish and then licked the lovely vanilla and cinnamon off the spoon the way she liked to eat it. While she was doing this, she looked anxiously over at the Endicott house and thought about her plan.

Her heart pounded. The Endicotts were at home. She knew this because their car was parked out front. She would go over and pay them a visit. She would say, "I just came to say hello." Could anything be wrong with that? She had the feeling there might well be something wrong with it because she had avoided mentioning this plan to her mother, even though she had made it up last night long before she kissed her mother good night and took her bath and went to bed.

It would be easier to say hello if Mr. Endicott

happened to come out into his yard. She waited a whole half hour after she finished the custard, but Mr. Endicott did not appear. Setting her chin firmly, she went out the back door, walked around her house, crossed over to the Endicotts' front yard, and knocked on the front door. Mrs. Endicott opened it.

Arms rigidly at her sides, Marcy said, "I just came to say hello."

"Oh?" Mrs. Endicott replied. And then, remembering her manners, her plump face brightened into the loveliest of smiles. "Well, now, isn't that nice! You must be Marcy from next door. Come in, dear."

Relief and gratitude bulged in Marcy's throat, and ducking her head, she went inside and sat bolt upright on the green sofa just inside the front door. She could smell the aroma of a pipe. It overwhelmed her with a fragrance she could only describe as delicious. From down in the basement came the most excellent whistling. She didn't know the tune, but the whistle was strong, clear, excellent.

She looked at Mrs. Endicott. "Is Mr. Endicott at home, too?" she inquired politely.

"Oh?" Again Mrs. Endicott seemed to remember her manners. "Yes. Yes, certainly. Excuse me." She hurried to the back of the house while Marcy's eyes swept the room. She could tell Mr. Endicott's chair. It was the gold one with the jar of pipe tobacco on the table beside it and the newspapers and a copy of the *Reader's Digest*.

"Dear, we have a visitor," Mrs. Endicott was calling.

"A visitor!" Mr. Endicott replied.

Marcy squeezed her eyes tight shut and instantly opened them again. She always did this when she was nervous. She knew Dr. Marvin had told her mother not to tell Marcy to stop this, but both Marcy and her mother wished she would. Marcy hoped she wouldn't start doing it a lot right now. It was Mrs. Endicott's calling her a visitor, leading Mr. Endicott to expect too much, that started it.

Then she heard his steps on the stairs, heavy and firm, almost making the house fall down, and he came into the living room, filling it with his bigness.

"Well, well! Marcy!" he said, and he smiled and winked, just as he had yesterday. Marcy felt she would explode.

"I just came to say hello," she said. She wished she had thought up more things to say than this. And then she remembered things she had heard

her mother say over the telephone and added, "I hope you will be very happy in your new home. Glenview is a small community and friendly."

"Well, well, that's certainly mighty good to hear," Mr. Endicott said, and Mrs. Endicott said, "Would you like some milk and cookies?"

She felt her eyes squeeze tight shut and open again. She didn't know what to say. She was full from the vanilla custard, but on the other hand...

"Of course she'd like milk and cookies," Mr. Endicott decided for her. "And I'd like a beer. Come on, Marcy." He held out his hand.

Quickly Marcy jumped off the sofa. Mr. Endicott's hand was big and warm and rough, and the wool shirt he wore was scratchy and wonderful. She took a little skip as they went through the dining room and into the kitchen. Mr. Endicott opened the refrigerator and set out a carton of milk and a bottle of beer. Mrs. Endicott put cookies on a plate and poured milk into a glass. Then they all sat down at the kitchen table.

"What school do you go to, Marcy?" said Mrs. Endicott.

"Kingswood Elementary."

"What grade are you in?"

"Fourth."

"That's real nice," said Mrs. Endicott.

Now nobody could think of anything more to say, so Marcy swallowed some milk and watched Mr. Endicott pour his beer, beautiful and pale yellow with cold foam on the top. Even if Marcy hadn't known, she would have guessed Mr. Endicott liked beer. Her mother seldom drank, and when she did, she liked sherry. Her mother always said, "Just a little bit of sherry, please." Marcy imagined Mrs. Endicott would say that, too.

Mr. Endicott said, "Libby, I got my gear sorted out downstairs so I can get your pictures hung up." He looked at Marcy. "You want to help me hang pictures?"

"Yes," Marcy answered.

It was very interesting helping Mr. Endicott hang pictures. After he hung the first one, Marcy got onto it and was careful to have the hammer or yardstick all ready to hand to him. When he found out where Mrs. Endicott wanted a picture, he would measure down from the ceiling and make a small mark with a stubby pencil. Then he would measure from the side and make a mark. Then he would select the right-size picture hanger from the handful Marcy held. He got the pictures on the wall in exactly the right spot

every time. Sometimes he whistled and sometimes he made little hissing noises through his
teeth, and once he clamped his hand down on
Marcy's head and said, "You're a real good help-
er, Marcy."

When it was time for her to be leaving, she told
him, "If there is anything you need me to help
with, I can come back tomorrow."

"Well, now, that's real nice of you, Marcy."

She hesitated, wondering if she might ask what
else needed doing, but she lost her nerve.

That night at supper her mother said, "What
did you do this afternoon, dear?"

"Oh, I just knocked around," Marcy said.

Chapter 2

The next afternoon after school, Marcy ate the piece of applesauce cake her mother had left in the refrigerator for her. Then she went out into her backyard and sat in the rope swing that hung from the pear tree. She wasn't quite sure what she should do. She had told Mr. Endicott she could come back and help him, and he had said that was real nice. Did that mean that he wanted her to come back or not?

She scuffed her shoes in the loose dirt under

the swing and twirled around a few times, letting the rope twist tight and then spin out, but she didn't do it too much because afterward it made her feel sick. Mostly, she kept looking at the back door of the Endicotts' house, and pretty soon it opened and Mr. Endicott came out. He didn't see her, though. He didn't even look over. He simply stood in the center of his yard and stared at it. Marcy got off the swing and crossed to the edge of her own yard. There was a bush there so anyone could see where her yard stopped and the Endicotts' yard started. "Hi, Mr. Endicott," she said.

He looked up. "Oh, hi, Marcy. How're you today?"

"Fine." She waited. She could say something like *Need any help today?* but Mr. Endicott seemed engrossed in thought. He seemed to have completely forgotten her. She turned and started toward her house. Then Mr. Endicott called, "Hey, Marcy, look at this now!"

Whirling around, she ran across to his yard, to where he was standing by the bush. "Look what I found," he said. "It's a purple martin house." He held up a battered wooden bird house with lots of small round holes in it. "I believe I can just fix this up and get it all nice and clean and maybe a

Mr. and Mrs. Martin will start eating our mosquitoes for us this summer."

"Is that what they eat?"

"Yep. A purple martin will eat its weight in bugs every day. I had a martin house in Jersey, but I never did entice a martin. Once I almost

did. This Mr. and Mrs. Martin came along, and they went flying in and out of all the little holes just like they were apartment hunting, but I guess my house didn't suit because they flew away."

"I certainly hope you'll be able to entice martins here," Marcy said.

"Yep. Have to get me a flagpole to set it on, though. Want to go down to the hardware store with me?"

Marcy hesitated. She was supposed to check in with her mother's office if she wanted to go anywhere, but Mr. Endicott already had his car keys out.

"Yes," she said, and fell into step beside him.

Mr. Endicott, Marcy observed as they drove into town, was an expert driver. Sitting on the seat beside him, Marcy knew she could just relax. Being in real estate her mother drove a lot. She had never had an accident, but she always frowned when she was driving and tightened her jaw. When her mother drove her places, Marcy frowned and tightened her jaw, too. But Mr. Endicott just drove nice and easy and sure of himself. Marcy let the cool air blow against her face and enjoyed herself.

At the hardware store, they spent quite a while

just looking at things. Marcy had never dreamed hardware stores could be so interesting. Mr. Endicott told her the names of a lot of things: hacksaws, molly bolts, planes, drill bits. You couldn't fool Mr. Endicott about any of them. Just the way he picked them up and held them in his hands, you knew he could do something with them. Then he ordered a flagpole and an iron pipe to set it in, and he told the clerk about his martin house. Marcy couldn't explain it, but just standing beside Mr. Endicott while he discussed his martin house made her feel good. Then the clerk looked at Marcy and said, "Your little girl going to help you get it up?"

"Yep," Mr. Endicott said and winked down at Marcy.

The next day was Saturday, and Marcy was going to Elizabeth Henderson's birthday party. On a chair beside her bed her mother had laid out her clothes: white tights, black patent leather shoes, her best petticoat, and her dark blue flowered cotton. The night before her mother had washed her hair. Aunt Peg would come to pick her up and take her to the party along with Wendy, her own little girl, because Saturday was a busy day in real estate for her mother.

In the morning, Marcy went over to the Endicotts' and knocked on the back screen door. Mr. Endicott called out, "It's open for you. Come right in." Then she went down to the cellar and helped Mr. Endicott nail the bird house back together and paint it white with a green roof. Mr. Endicott let her paint a little of the roof, and it was just perfect. Afterward, she went home, ate the bologna sandwich her mother had left her, put on her party clothes, took the puzzle her mother had wrapped up in pink and white paper, and waited on her porch for Aunt Peg.

It was coming back from the party that Marcy made her big mistake. They were all in Aunt Peg's car; not only Wendy and Marcy, but Carolyn Bingham and Evie Tyce and Susan Hackley. They got talking about birds, and before Marcy realized it, she had said, "This morning my father and I made a purple martin house."

Nobody paid any attention at all. Nobody even noticed it, except Aunt Peg. Aunt Peg quickly looked over her shoulder right at Marcy.

The next day Marcy decided that maybe Aunt Peg hadn't noticed it either, because Marcy knew that if Aunt Peg had noticed, she would tell Marcy's mother. But Marcy's mother didn't act any different. She just dropped Marcy off at Sunday school and then went off to the office.

While Marcy was in Sunday school, it began to rain hard. It hadn't even looked like rain when her mother dropped her at the church door. When Sunday school was over, people came for their children. Most of them were fathers. They opened up umbrellas and held them way over their daughters' heads even if they got wet themselves. Evie Tyce's father said, "Come along, Marcy. I'll give you a lift home." He tried to keep both Evie and Marcy under the umbrella, but this was hard to do, so mostly he held the umbrella over Evie, which was understandable.

At home Marcy changed her clothes and ate the peanut butter and jelly sandwich her mother had left her. While she ate it, she looked out the window, but not into the Endicotts' kitchen where the Endicotts were having their Sunday dinner. She looked out at the purple martin house now perched on top of the flagpole, hoping the paint was good and dry. Then the telephone rang. It was Mr. Endicott.

"Hi, Marcy," he said. "Libby made brown Betty for desert. Would you like some?"

"Yes," Marcy answered.

"All right. Just hold onto your hat. I'll come over for you."

Mr. Endicott came to the back door with a big

black umbrella. As they crossed the yard, he held it carefully over Marcy even though he got wet. Marcy found she was closing her eyes tight and opening them instantly. This surprised her. She hadn't known she would do this if she was glad.

Chapter 3

Sunday night was the best night of the week because her mother never had to go to the office on Monday and so they could celebrate. Every Sunday night they went to Carswell's Restaurant to eat dinner. Usually her mother ordered roast lamb and a baked potato. Marcy always ordered spaghetti. For dessert they both always had pound cake and vanilla ice cream and hot fudge sauce. Mr. and Mrs. Carswell usually came to their table to say hello, and Marcy and her mother knew all the waitresses. A pink electric light glowed in the fireplace under logs that looked like real wood. It was nice. When they got home this particular Sunday night, her mother said, "Marcy, where did you go in the rain today? I was worried when you didn't answer the phone."

Marcy didn't look at her mother. "I went over to the Endicotts' for some brown Betty. I was invited," she added quickly.

"The Endicotts'?" her mother said, raising her eyebrows. "You aren't supposed to go anywhere unless you check in with me. You know that, Marcy."

"This was just next door."

"That doesn't matter. You must check in with me. You know that very well."

Marcy did know this very well. Somehow she also knew that Aunt Peg had tattled, so she said, "Yesterday morning I was at the Endicotts', too. I helped make a purple martin house."

"Then there really is a purple martin house?" her mother cried. She sounded so relieved that Marcy looked at her in surprise.

"Of course," Marcy said. "Mr. Endicott put it on a flagpole in the backyard."

"Ohhhh," her mother said, as though she understood a great mystery.

The next day when Marcy got home from school her mother wasn't in the house, which was strange because it was Monday. Then Marcy looked out the window and saw her standing in the Endicotts' backyard talking to Mr. and Mrs. Endicott. What was even more strange was to see her mother reach down into her pocket, pull out a tissue, wipe her eyes, and blow her nose. Her mother was crying — crying in front of the Endicotts who were smiling! As Marcy watched, Mrs. Endicott patted her mother's arm. Then her mother turned and was walking back to the house, and though she was still dabbing at her eyes, she was smiling, too.

"What was all that about?" Marcy asked sternly when her mother came in the back door.

"Oh, you're home," her mother said.

"Yes. Why were you crying?"

She could tell her mother felt caught out and was trying to think up an answer. "The Endicotts are lovely, lovely people," her mother said.

"But why were you crying?" Marcy persisted relentlessly.

"That is a private matter."

Marcy would remember that answer for future

use, although her mother usually always knew why Marcy was crying and so never had to ask.

"The Endicotts are very fond of you, Marcy," her mother said. "But I hope you won't outwear your welcome. And always be polite."

It was permission! Permission to visit the Endicotts as much as she liked. And she hadn't even asked.

After that Monday, Marcy looked in on the Endicotts every day that she didn't have to go somewhere else, like to Wendy's house. If she had to go somewhere else, she always phoned Mr. Endicott the night before and told him. This was because the first time she didn't turn up after school, Mr. Endicott had gotten worried and had gone down to Kingswood Elementary to look for her and then had phoned her mother at Barton Realty.

Marcy was very polite and never wore out her welcome because she could always tell the days Mr. Endicott wouldn't mind if she knocked around after him and the days it would be better just to say hello and go back home. The Endicotts always left their back screen door unlatched for her. It was never locked even once.

"Marcy, you're doing better," Miss Mac-Mannes said one day, handing back her composition. "Much, much better, although your spelling must improve."

On top of the paper Miss MacMannes had written *Very good*. It was the first *Very good* Marcy had ever received. Carefully she flattened the paper inside her geography book, and when she went over to the Endicotts' that afternoon, she showed it to Mr. Endicott. She was embarrassed by the big circles Miss MacMannes had put around the misspelled words, but Mr. Endicott didn't seem to notice them. "Why it says here *Very good*," he said. And then he sat down at the kitchen table with his beer and read it. While he read it, Marcy hooked her arm over his shoulder and read it, too.

THE MARTIN HOUSSE
by
Marcia Benson

Today my father and I found an old martin housse. Perple martins eat their wate in mes mus bugs every day. My father fixed up the housse and he put it on a flag pole. Now my father and I are waiting for martins to move in. The End.

After he read it, Mr. Endicott took out his handkerchief and blew his nose. "I can certainly see why Miss MacMannes said it's very good," he said.

"You can keep it if you want," Marcy said. She wasn't sure he understood so she whispered, "It's sort of about us."

"I can see that," Mr. Endicott said. "And I would certainly like to keep it. But you should show it to your mom first."

When she showed it to her mother that night, her mother paid attention to the misspelled words. She made Marcy spell *house* and *purple* and *weight*. She even made her spell *mosquito*. Then she said, "It's very good, Marcy. It's a very nice story. Isn't it fun to make things up?"

"It's not made up," Marcy said firmly. "It's true."

Her mother frowned. She had a worried look like whenever Marcy ran a fever. "It's all right to pretend, Marcy. As long as you remember you're only pretending," she said.

Marcy snatched up the paper and went into the other room.

Chapter 4

The Endicotts did their shopping early on Saturday mornings. Until the Endicotts moved in, Marcy's mother always arranged for Marcy to visit around on Saturday because she said Saturday was too long a day for Marcy to be all alone. If she couldn't arrange to drop Marcy off somewhere, she gave her money to go to the kids' show at the Rialto on Main Street. All this was O.K., but most times Marcy would have preferred to just knock around the house and look at the TV instead of always having to go somewhere.

After the Endicotts moved in, Saturdays got better. The Endicotts just naturally got into the habit of taking Marcy shopping with them. It wasn't easy to get the habit started because the Endicotts had to convince and convince Marcy's mother that they really liked having Marcy along and that she was never any trouble — as though Marcy herself wouldn't rather die than cause trouble for the Endicotts.

Quite the contrary. Her mother might not realize it, but Marcy was ever on the alert to be helpful. On Saturday morning she would arrive just as the Endicotts were having their second cup of coffee. Sometimes she had a cup also, heavily laced with milk, but usually she went immediately to work, getting the kitchen shears out of the drawer and spreading out the weekly flyer from Monsanto's Quality Super Market on the kitchen floor.

Monsanto's did an interesting job on their flyers. For instance, the offer of

Firm Ripe   *pkg. of*
Slicing Tomatoes   *3*   *25¢*

was accompanied by a picture of three small

plump tomatoes with sprinkles of water on them. Just looking at them made you want to bite into them.

Cookie Specials!!

featured a large barrel heaped to the top and overflowing with saved dollar bills.

The savings on most items were astonishing. Marcy always looked first for the saving earned by the extra Super Bonus coupon. But as she worked away with the scissors, she gave close attention to all the coupons, the ones the Endicotts had marked with an X and the ones they hadn't. Sometimes she was able to bring special savings to their attention; items they themselves had missed.

"By George, Marcy, you paid for the gas with that one," Mr. Endicott would say. "That's because you keep your eyes peeled."

Since Marcy had made the acquaintance of Mr. Endicott, she had developed the habit of keeping her eyes peeled. Lots of things she never paid any attention to before, she caught quick as a wink now: things like net weight, and thirty-two fluid ounces being a quart, and whether the large economy size was really all that much of a big saving or not. Often Mr. Endicott would let her click off prices with his pocket calculator.

After they finished at Monsanto's, there were other errands. Sometimes Mrs. Endicott needed a zipper or more writing paper. While Mrs. Endicott went to the Singer Center or the five and dime, Marcy and Mr. Endicott would shove off for Sears. Sometimes Mr. Endicott would buy a little box of tacks or maybe a spool of copper wire, but mostly they just looked over the hand tool

section, picking things up and putting them down, feeling the weight of them, running a hand over them. Always they stood and admired the electric table saw, and always Mr. Endicott said the same thing: "I'd buy one of them if only I had the use for it."

The last thing they did was go to the bakery. All three of them went to the bakery because, as Mr. Endicott said, just walking to Burger's Bakery was a pleasure of pure delight. And on Saturday morning it was at its best: trays heaped with donuts, sugared or glazed or stuffed with whipped cream; shelves loaded with pies and cinnamon buns (plain or cashew) and a fine display of Danish. Slowly they moved from counter to counter considering each possibility, and then Mrs. Endicott would say, "I'd like a half dozen plain cinnamon buns, a loaf of rye bread, and three sugar donuts, please." Mrs. Endicott detested rye bread, but Mr. Endicott liked it, so she always bought it for him. Driving home they would each eat a sugar donut. It was fun.

Coming home one Saturday, they met Mr. Parry, the mailman, outside Endicotts'. He gave the Endicotts their mail and gave Marcy the Benson mail. Marcy looked at the letter on top, and her heart did a quick flip. It was addressed to

Mrs. Janet Benson, 9 Morris Avenue, Glenview, Pa. 18924. It was postmarked Los Angeles, and in the upper left-hand corner was: Mr. John Benson, Oriole Way, Los Angeles, Calif. 90077. The letter felt thin, almost as though there was nothing in it at all, and for some reason Marcy felt shaky and queer.

"I guess I'll go home now," she said.

"Okie doke, Marcy. Be seein' you," Mr. Endicott said.

She went around to her back door and fitted the key in the lock and opened the door. Then she put the letter down on the kitchen counter and all the junk mail and stuff to one side. She couldn't tell anything about the handwriting because Mr. John Benson, her father, had used a typewriter, but still she stared at it, all the time feeling queer inside. Then she turned it over and looked at the back of the envelope, but there wasn't anything written on the back, so she turned it face up again and went up to her room and sat on the edge of her bed.

She had really forgotten she had an actual father. She never thought of him at all any more. She hadn't seen him since she was a little, little girl and now, of all things, a letter! A letter from California. She tried to imagine California and the Pacific Ocean, but instead she kept seeing Atlantic City and the boardwalk and the Atlantic Ocean. Then she tried to imagine her father.

Once she had some pictures of him. Not many, but some. She had kept them in an envelope in the bottom of her dresser drawer. It irked her now that only last year she had thrown them away. She had needed more space for clothes, so she had cleared out the old junk in the dresser drawer — stuff she knew she would never use again: a ping-pong paddle she had found on top of somebody's trash can, some rocks, comic books, junk like that. She hadn't been sure what to do about the pictures, so she had asked her mother.

"What do you want to do about them?" her mother had asked.

"I don't know," she answered. "I guess I may as well throw them away."

Her mother had hesitated and then said, "You may be sorry about that some day, Marcy. Why don't you just tuck them in your desk?"

"Because I want to throw them away," Marcy had snapped. And right at that moment she had wanted to get rid of them in the worst possible way. She had felt glad and relieved when she tossed them in the trash can and even better after the trash man had carted the trash away. But, as usual, her mother had been right. Now she was sorry. She couldn't really remember what her father looked like at all. And it certainly made her mad that her mother always had to be so darn right all the time.

The telephone rang. Her heart leaped and the palms of her hands got sweaty. Could it be... well, just possibly, it could be her father. It rang again. She didn't want to answer it if it was going to be her father. But more likely it was her mother, and if she didn't answer, her mother would be anxious all afternoon. At the third ring, she ran down the hall to her mother's bedroom and picked up the receiver. It was Carolyn Bingham wanting to know if Marcy was going to the Rialto that afternoon. Marcy said she was.

"So am I," said Carolyn. "I'll meet you by the popcorn machine."

"O.K.," said Marcy. "But guess what?"

"What?"

"My mother got a letter from my father in California today."

"And...?" said Carolyn.

"Nothing," said Marcy, beginning to feel foolish. "Just that she got a letter."

"So what's the big deal? My father writes to my mother all the time when he's away. He writes to me, too."

"Sure."

"Well, I mean, so what's the big deal?" Carolyn persisted.

"No big deal."

"Wow! You sound like you've flipped!"

"I'll see you at the Rialto," said Marcy.

When Marcy got home from the movies, her mother wasn't home yet, so she went into the house and looked at the letter on the kitchen counter. Then she went into the backyard and sat on the swing and pressed her tongue against the loose tooth she had. She liked the pain of pressing her tongue against it. It took her mind off the letter. But as soon as her mother drove into the garage at the end of the backyard, she jumped off the swing and followed her into the house.

Her mother didn't even glance at the kitchen counter. She dumped all her packages down by the sink and began saying how she'd bought some nice Swiss cheese and some beautiful apples and stuff like that, all the while handing Marcy two cartons of milk and a box of eggs and the other things they stored in the refrigerator.

When her mother finished doing that, right away she slit open a package of dried beef and began to make supper. Marcy could stand the suspense no longer.

"Today you got a letter," she said.

"Who from?" asked her mother, not even looking around.

"Mr. John Benson, Los Angeles, California."

That did it! Right away her mother spun around.

With satisfaction, Marcy said, "It's there — right there under your nose on the kitchen counter."

"Don't talk fresh, Marcy," said her mother. She went to the counter, picked up the letter with scarcely a glance, and put it in her apron pocket. Then she went back to slicing up the dried beef as though nothing had happened.

Marcy was astonished. "Aren't you going to read it?"

"Later."

"Why not now?"

"*Because* I *prefer* to read it *later*."

Disregarding the tone of her mother's voice, Marcy said, "Are you going to tell me what he has to say?"

"That depends."

Marcy was really stepping on thin ice now, but she just had to. "Depends on what?"

That, too, did it. Again her mother spun around. "On whether it concerns you, Marcy! And it's not right to question others about their mail. Hand me the milk carton, please."

Marcy got out the milk carton, set it down hard by the stove, turned, and left the room.

Chapter 5

Occasionally on Saturday night her mother went out. If she was going out, Marcy slept overnight at Wendy's house or some other place. But usually her mother read the paper after supper and then turned on the TV, and they watched a couple of shows and had Fritos and Pepsi and went to bed.

But that night after supper her mother only pretended to read the paper. Her mother didn't fool Marcy one bit. She kept turning over the pages and turning them back again, but her mind was elsewhere, plain as day. At last, she folded the paper, stuck it under the end table, and said, "Your father's note does concern you, Marcy. He has remarried. His wife's name is Virginia. He would like to have Virginia meet you. They will arrive here in two weeks, and they would like to take you into Philadelphia for the weekend."

For a long moment, Marcy stared at her mother while this astonishing information sank in. Then she said, "Why do they want to take me to Philadelphia?"

"Because they think it will be pleasant for you, I expect."

"But I don't like cities."

"Yes, Marcy, but of course they don't know that. And anyway, it's been several years since you've been in a city. You may find you like it now."

Marcy's eyes began blinking so fast that she couldn't count the blinks. "Will you be coming, too?"

"No, baby. But I'll be right here waiting for you when you get back."

It was calling her *baby,* which her mother seldom did anymore, and her voice being so nice and all, that made Marcy's chin tremble and the tears start. "I don't have to go, do I?" she choked. Leaping from her chair, she grabbed her mother's chin in her hands, and stooping so that her face was right up against her mother's, she begged, "Don't make me go, Mom. Please don't make me go! I don't know him. I don't remember him. I'll get sick. Throw up!" And then an even worse possibility occurred to her and she screamed, "Mom! Mom, maybe they won't bring me back!"

"Marcy...! Of course they'll bring you back."

"How do you *know*?"

"Because of the law, Marcy."

Marcy caught her breath. "The law?"

"Here, Marcy. Sit here," her mother said, and Marcy was astonished to find herself sitting in her mother's lap with her mother's arms around her, pressing her to her softness. They hadn't done this since she was a little girl.

"Now, Marcy, I want to explain to you how it is," she said quietly. "When your father and I were divorced, a court of law gave me sole custody of you. It usually happens that way. Usually the mother gets custody of the children and the father has the right to visit them. But he can never, never take them anywhere, not even for a weekend, unless the mother says it's O.K. And if he ever did try to take them away, then all over the

44

country the police would be alerted, and they would find the children and bring them straight back home and put the father in jail. So now just tell me what would be the sense in your father's doing something like that?"

Marcy let out a shuddering sigh. She felt relieved because obviously her father would not be bothered going through anything like that just to land in jail, especially when he was just married and everything.

"And anyway," her mother continued, "your father wouldn't dream of doing anything like that. I'm sure he and his wife will do everything they can to make this little jaunt a real treat for you. I bet you'll be sorry when it's over."

"I won't," Marcy said. "Because I'll throw up."

Her mother sighed. "I doubt that, Marcy. You'll have too many things to see and do to think about your stomach. But if you feel like you're going to throw up, simply excuse yourself and go to the ladies' room."

"But what if we're driving in the car or something?"

"Goodness, Marcy! Then simply ask your father to stop the car."

Marcy could tell her mother was getting out of patience, and she didn't blame her. She also had begun to feel like some kind of nut sitting there on her lap, so she climbed off. But she still didn't want to go with her father! She didn't want to go at all. And somehow she would simply have to think of a way to get out of it.

The perfect solution came smack in the middle of Monday morning in Miss MacMannes's fourth grade in the Kingswood Elementary School. It came because Michael Knight stood inside the mock-up of a TV set that Grade Four had made and read his composition on dental health. While he read it, Marcy lounged at the round table she shared with Evie Tyce and Mary Elliott and Wendy and kind of poked around her loose tooth with her tongue. It was getting looser, all right, and the plan was to keep working on it and finally poke it out.

But right in the middle of a long, hard, pleasantly painful push, she stopped and drew her tongue away. She had it! She wouldn't touch her tooth anymore. She would be careful not to let even water get to that side. She would save that tooth for two weeks and then, on that Saturday morning when her father came, she would complain about her awful toothache and have to go to Dr. Ketterman right away for an emergency extraction. Afterward she would have to come home and lie down and rest like she did once before. She shuddered a bit at the thought of Dr. Ketterman pulling another tooth, but she had no doubt whatsoever that she preferred the brief pain of an extraction to The Weekend.

The relief was so great that when Miss Mac-Mannes said, "Marcy, what did you think of Michael's composition?" Marcy answered, "I think it was the best composition I ever heard."

"Really!" Miss MacMannes exclaimed. "What did you like about it?"

"It was so good, I guess," Marcy faltered.

But Miss MacMannes clearly had no intention of letting up. "You think it was good, yes," she said approvingly. "But good in what way?"

"I just liked it," Marcy stumbled on, aware now that she hadn't paid much attention to Michael at all.

"But liked it *how*, Marcy? Did you like the organization? Or the presentation? The choice of words, perhaps? The subject matter?"

Marcy pounced on the statement that might be considered true. "The subject matter!"

Miss MacMannes smiled. She had a lovely smile and wore neat pantsuits, and Marcy really liked her a lot. "So dental health interests you, does it, Marcy?" she inquired warmly. "Well, that's splendid! If you keep your interest, you might one day become a dentist!" She turned to the class. "Class, what other career might Marcy pursue if she maintains her interest in dental health?"

Everyone started commenting on her future in dentistry. It was awful!

David Tully said she could make false teeth and all kinds of things like that, which made Marcy positively sick. Ilona Greenawald said this was called being a dental technician, but that she might also become an oral surgeon or a dental nurse or a receptionist in a dentist's office.

Connie Adams commented that Marcy's interest in dental health would be good if she decided she wanted to get married and raise children because she would know what to do about her husband's teeth and her children's teeth and even her own.

Miss MacMannes said, "Connie, that is a very good point because diet is important in the care and health of the teeth, and certainly an interest in dental health would make Marcy a better mother." Then she turned again to Marcy with her lovely smile. "Well, Marcy! You haven't been able to think what to do for your special science project. I'd like to suggest that you make up a booklet on dental health. Now what do you think of *that* suggestion!"

Miss MacMannes looked so pleased that Marcy couldn't bear to disappoint her. Anyway, she figured she somehow deserved it. "Sure, Miss MacMannes," she said.

At recess Wendy said suspiciously, "You never told me you were all that interested in dental health."

Wendy was her best friend. Marcy had to at least try to be honest with Wendy. "Well, it's more like I'm not against it."

"Not against it!" cried Wendy. "I'm not against it either, but I certainly wouldn't want to spend my life pulling out people's rotten old teeth and smelling their breath and..."

"Wendy, stop it!" cried Marcy. "You're making me sick!"

Wendy had a way of saying Awwwk! and swallowing hard twice and banging her ears if she simply couldn't believe what she heard. She did this now. "Awwwk!" Swallow, swallow; bang, bang. "How do you expect to *do* it if you can't even *talk* about it?"

"That's *just* the problem!" Marcy said haughtily and walked away.

Chapter 6

Marcy would never have believed it was so difficult to keep her tongue away from that loose tooth. Despite her best efforts, the very minute she stopped thinking about it her tongue would skip over and give it a good push. Each morning, first thing, she would feel for it, and each night she would thank God for one more successful day and beg Him to keep watch over it and not let her push it out in her sleep.

The whole thing was just exhausting, and it

wasn't helped by all her mother's activity. Every single night her mother would come home, eat supper, and then start washing windows and ironing curtains and even taking out silver ash trays and candlesticks and copper-bottomed pots and pans that Marcy hadn't seen for years and polishing them and sticking them around in places.

"What are you doing all this junk for?" Marcy demanded irritably.

"Because I've got my pride, is why," her mother said. "When your father and his wife walk in, this place is going to look absolutely A-1 perfect."

"That's just dumb," Marcy said.

"In your view," replied her mother. "And don't talk fresh to me, Marcy."

The whole thing was sickening, but one thing sure, Marcy absolutely refused new clothes.

"For the life of me I can't understand why you don't want a nice new spring suit to wear into Philadelphia," her mother would say. She would say it over and over again.

Marcy wished that she could say, "Because I won't be going to Philadelphia. I'll be having my extraction." She wished she could let her mother in on the plan, but that would only mean disaster. Her mother had already said a couple of hundred times, "Now, Marcy, I want you to take care you don't catch cold or anything so you'll be feeling well for The Weekend."

Her mother made Marcy mad. In fact, it seemed Marcy was mad at everything. She was mad at her mother and mad at the house looking so darn clean and awful. And then the worst possible thing happened. She got mad at Mr. Endicott!

It was the Wednesday night before The Weekend, and she had gone over to the Endicotts' because Mr. Endicott had phoned to say he had found some dental health pictures in a magazine. She hated that stupid dental health project. She even hated Miss MacMannes for suggesting it, but she was sure glad to get out of the house where her mother was waxing the kitchen floor, of all things!

It was a big relief to go down to the Endicotts' basement, where Mr. Endicott was sanding a rocking chair for Mrs. Endicott. Marcy sat on his high work stool and watched him work. It was peaceful sitting there with the radio turned on low and watching Mr. Endicott rub the chair with the finest grade sandpaper until, when you stroked it, the wood felt like satin.

Sometimes, when they were alone like this, they talked. Sometimes they didn't. Either way, it didn't matter, and if Marcy was supposed to go into Philadelphia for The Weekend with Mr. and Mrs. Endicott instead of her father and his new wife, everything would be just perfect.

"I wish I was supposed to go into Philadelphia with you and Mrs. Endicott instead of my father and his new wife."

Mr. Endicott looked up from his work. Then he began sanding again. "Well, now, Marcy," he said, "the feeling I have is that it may not be so bad as you expect. That's the way things usually turn out, more often than not. You can dread doing a thing something fierce, and then when you start doing it, it doesn't seem like it's so bad after all."

Marcy appreciated that Mr. Endicott didn't try to tell her The Weekend was going to be "just wonderful," a trick Wendy's mother had tried to pull a couple of times. It was because of this that she decided to try something out on him.

"I don't think I'm going to go with them," she said slowly.

Mr. Endicott didn't say anything. He just kept sanding away, so she said louder, "I said I don't think I'm going to go with them."

"I heard what you said the first time. I'm just trying to frame a careful answer."

This made Marcy madder than she had been with anyone. "I don't want you to frame a careful answer! I just don't think I'm going to go, that's all."

Mr. Endicott straightened up and put down his sandpaper. He looked right into her eyes until she couldn't stand looking back at him anymore and had to look down at the cement floor.

"You're nervous about it. I can understand that. But I'll bet your father feels a little bit nervous, too, driving all the way from California with his new wife just to see you," Mr. Endicott said. "I'll bet he's hoping and hoping everything will go just fine. I'll bet he's got all sorts of plans he hopes will go off real well. Now all you have to do is be nice and polite and say, 'Yes, sir,' and 'Yes, ma'am,' and pretty soon you'll get to know him. You even may get to like him a little."

At this, Marcy's head shot up. "I never will!"

"Why not?"

"Because he's never come to see me all these years, that's why! Because I don't want him to be my father at all!"

It was then it happened. Marcy hadn't realized it, but all this time she had been pushing harder and harder on her loose tooth. With a final push, it fell out. For a minute she couldn't figure what was in her mouth, and then, with awful certainty, she knew.

Tears stung her eyes, and, choking, she spit the tooth into her hands. Shoving it under Mr. Endicott's nose, she cried, "Now look what you made me do! You've wrecked it! You've wrecked everything! I hate you!"

Turning from his puzzled face, she stumbled up the basement stairs and out the Endicotts' back door.

Chapter 7

The next day Marcy's mother took off from work and picked her up at school and took her to Fisher's for a new spring suit. If her mother didn't care that she might throw up on a perfectly new suit, why should Marcy? And there certainly was no way of getting out of The Weekend now. Mr. Endicott had fixed that, all right. But good!

She tried to look with dull disinterest at the reflection of herself in Fisher's mirror, but she had to admit that the short pink wool skirt and pink jacket with round brass buttons down the front and on each cuff were very nice. One other thought brought a small comfort. Before she went to school that morning, she had carefully washed off her tooth and put it in her jewel box. She intended to tape it to a piece of red construction paper. She'd draw black lightning streaks of pain around it. It would be the cover for her dental health project. The effect would be spectacular.

On Friday night, her mother washed Marcy's hair and scrubbed and clipped her nails, even her toenails! Next her mother packed a new black patent leather overnight bag with a new pair of green-sprigged pajamas and new green scuffs and a toothbrush. The toothbrush was the only thing old in the entire enterprise. Marcy told her mother it was all a ridiculous expense.

"In your view," her mother answered.

"Not only in my view," Marcy said severely. "In any person's view because I'll never use that patent leather bag again."

"You'll use it for overnights."

"I will not! You know I carry my gear in a paper bag. You know that."

"Then you'll use it for college."

"College!"

Her mother had this one failing. She always had to have an answer. She could never be wrong.

"Yes, college," her mother said. "And even after college. You'll find you'll have many uses for it over the years."

"I will not."

"Wait and see."

There it was again, that failing. Her mother just always had to be right.

When Marcy climbed into bed, she was sure she wouldn't sleep a wink. She thought of the astronauts and how Walter Cronkite always said they had a good night's sleep before lift-off. *This morning, after a good night's sleep....* Then he would describe what they ate for breakfast. The astronauts always ate huge breakfasts. Marcy had already decided she wouldn't eat breakfast at all because you couldn't throw up if you had nothing to throw, but she certainly had no trouble getting to sleep. It didn't seem anytime before her mother was saying as she always said, "Come on, Marcy. Rise and shine."

Chapter 8

Because Marcy had been thoughtless enough to throw away those old photos, she had no idea what to expect her father to look like. She sat in the living room on the sofa all dressed up in her new pink suit, with her new black patent leather bag beside her, and blinked her eyes.

Her mother was making coffee in the kitchen, a big pot of fresh-perked coffee, not instant. It made it seem like Monday morning instead of Saturday because it was only on Monday that her mother took time for fresh coffee.

"You look beautiful, Marcy," her mother had said when Marcy got all dressed. "Perfectly beautiful." She gazed at her a long moment, taking in every part of her. "I'm very proud of my little girl." Then she turned around real fast and made a beeline for the kitchen.

When Marcy heard the car stop out front and then two car doors slam one after the other, her heart started hammering so hard that she thought it would come thundering right out of her body.

"Mom!" she called shrilly. "They're here!"

"I know," her mother said, instantly appearing. She must have been listening hard, too, all the way from the back of the house, and this was good because Marcy could never have answered the door. She didn't believe she could even stand up, let alone move.

Maybe her mother wouldn't be able to move either. Her mother stood perfectly rigid, and, scarcely breathing, they both listened to the footsteps coming up the front walk and then climbing the four wooden steps and then sounding on the porch. When the doorbell rang, they both jumped.

Then her mother kind of drifted to the front door and opened it.

"Hello, Johnnie," she said, and her voice was perfectly easy and calm. "How are you?"

"Fine, Janet! Just fine! Fine!"

Her father's voice was so booming and loud that Marcy thought they must probably hear him over at the Endicotts'! Then he said, "Janet, I'd like you to meet Ginny, here." Her mother said, "Hello," and a soft voice answered "Hello," and then her mother opened the door wide and said, "Come in, won't you?" and first her father's new wife came in and then her father.

In that first moment, the only impression of him that Marcy caught was that he was on the short side, powerfully built and very handsome, with blazing blue eyes and a suntan. He stood in the doorway, looking at her, and then he opened his arms and said, "Wow! Tiger! Tiger! Wow!"

"Marcy..." her mother prodded.

Unbelievably, Marcy found she could arise, and one foot followed the other over to her father.

Her father got down on one knee so that his face was right level with hers and she could look into his blazing blue eyes and smell his shaving cream. Then he took her hand. "Wow!" he said very softly, and crushed her in a bear hug.

After that, it was just as Mr. Endicott said. You could dread doing a thing something fierce and then, when you started doing it, it didn't seem so bad after all.

She had a Pepsi and everyone else had coffee and talked about California. Then her mother asked them if they would like to see the house, and she took them straight through it from top to bottom. Marcy was glad now that it looked so pretty with all the curtains washed and the kitchen floor waxed and the copper pots so shiny.

Then her father said they really should get a move on, so Marcy kissed her mother good-bye and went down the front walk carrying her black patent leather suitcase to the big bright yellow car standing at the curb. She hoped Mr. and Mrs. Endicott were looking out the window to see this. She wished there could be a whole big crowd around: Mr. Parry, the mailman, and Wendy and Aunt Peg and Evie Tyce and even Miss Mac-Mannes.

"Front or back, Tiger?" her father said.

"Why don't I sit in back, Johnnie?" said Virginia.

"O.K., Ginger," said her father.

It was funny the way her father had all these different names for people. Virginia was Ginger or Ginny and, once, Gin-Gin. Marcy, for some strange reason, was Tiger. And once, back in the house, he had called her mother *Cakes*, of all things, and gotten red under his suntan and quickly changed it to Janet.

Out on the highway, he turned the radio on and drove a little too fast for Marcy's liking. Every now and then he would take his eyes off the road to grin down at her and growl, "Hi, Tiger!"

Each time, Marcy would smile politely and say, "Hi!" but pretty soon he stopped doing this, and Marcy was grateful. She was grateful for something else, too. She somehow knew she was in absolutely no danger of throwing up.

"How was it?" Wendy asked as soon as recess was called on Monday morning. It was a chill, raw day and they stood with their hands in their jacket pockets kind of jigging on the cement playground.

"It was O.K.," Marcy told her.

"O.K. good? Or just O.K.?"

"O.K. good, I guess," Marcy answered. "They were nice to me. They want me to come to California and visit them this summer."

"Luckeee! Will your mom let you go?"

"If I want to."

Wendy did the Awwwk, swallow-swallow, bang-bang. "Don't tell me you don't want to!"

"I haven't made up my mind yet."

"Awwwk!" Wendy began again. It was even worse than *Hi, Tiger*.

One of the nice things about Mr. Endicott was that he didn't say things like *Awwwk!* or *Hi, Tiger*. He didn't even say things like *Did you remember to be polite and thank your father and Virginia?* the way her mother did. When Marcy told Mr. Endicott that The Weekend had been O.K., he simply said, "That's fine, Marcy. That's real fine."

Chapter 9

Working at the kitchen counter on her dental
health project, Marcy was surprised to realize she
was actually sorry to be finishing it up. Always
before, her projects had been slap-dash and care-
less. She hated projects and put them off until
the last minute. Then she would have to hunt
wildly through magazines for any old kind of pictures and paste them up any old way. But the
dental health project had been fun.

Right at the start, Mr. Endicott had given her

a large folder in which to keep the pictures she clipped. By the time she was ready to assemble the project, she had a whole stock from which to choose, all cut with a care for the edges. She was good at clipping things now, thanks to the practice with Monsanto's Quality Super Market coupons. When, finally, she got to the paste-up stage, she centered each picture using a ruler the way Mr. Endicott centered pictures on a wall. The effect was beautiful.

And the front cover . . . ! Mr. Endicott had given her two pieces of cardboard. She had carefully pasted a piece of red construction paper to one cardboard for the back cover. The front cover also had a piece of red construction paper over cardboard and, in the exact center, fixed in rubber cement, was her tooth.

It had been Mr. Endicott's idea to use the rubber cement. Marcy had been overjoyed with the suggestion because it certainly was better than covering the tooth all up with Scotch tape. She had only one regret. She wished the tooth were larger. But with all the zigzag pain lines running out from it, done not only in black crayon but also purple, green, and yellow, it looked fantastic! At the top of the cover, worked in the neatest block lettering, was the title: *Dental Health.* At the bottom, also neatly lettered, was her name: *Marcia Benson.*

After she had punched holes in the front and back covers and threaded red string through the whole thing, she sat back and spent five minutes just looking at it. She really hated to let it out of her sight. When she got it back from the Curriculum Fair, she intended to keep it forever.

The Curriculum Fair was a really big thing at Kingswood Elementary. It was held at night, for one thing, so everybody's parents could come. And all the rooms were open so you could walk around and see all the different projects and go in and visit any place you liked.

By the time Marcy and her mother arrived at the school on the night of the fair, things were really in full swing.

"Do you want to start at the pre-1 Room or do you want to start at the Fourth Grade?" Marcy asked.

"I'd like to go to the Fourth Grade first," her mother answered.

Marcy nodded with satisfaction.

Fourth Grade was really jam-pack-crowded. Everybody was there. Mr. and Mrs. Tyce, Mr. and Mrs. Bingham, Dr. and Mrs. Greenawald, and lots of parents Marcy didn't know. Around the walls hung the projects. Marcy's eyes slid quickly over them. She didn't want to appear to be looking for her own.

Over in a corner, Uncle David, Wendy's father, stood talking to Miss MacMannes. Marcy tried to imagine what it would be like if, instead of Uncle David, it was Johnnie standing over there talking to her teacher. She found she couldn't imagine this at all, so she gave it up.

Just then, Wendy spied them. "Marcy, have you seen yours?" she cried. "Aunt Janet, have you seen Marcy's?"

"No," said Marcy's mother.

"Follow me!" Wendy said importantly. She led them to Miss MacMannes's desk. The desk top had been swept clean of all the junk Miss Mac-Mannes usually kept on it, and there, displayed on the dictionary stand, was *Dental Health* by *Marcia Benson.* A blue ribbon had been stapled to the cover, and a white card rested against it. On the card, in capital letters, was typed one word: OUTSTANDING.

"It's the only *Outstanding* in the room," Wendy breathed.

Marcy stared at it. Then, without even realizing it, she said "Awwwk," swallowed twice, and banged her ears.

Chapter 10

Mr. Endicott was planting a garden down at the
end of his yard. Whistling between his teeth, he
measured out where each row would go and then
tapped in a stick. He did this all around the garden patch. Then he tied string to a far stick and
walked across the garden amd tied it to a front
stick. He did that to all the sticks in the garden,
and just looking at those rows of strings was a
beautiful sight in itself without anything growing
up to them.

He had tomato plants he was going to set out beside some poles so they could get support while they were growing and three raspberry bushes because Mrs. Endicott liked raspberries and cream, but the rest of the garden was for flowers: zinnias, asters, marigolds, snapdragons, and bachelor buttons because Mrs. Endicott liked flowers best of all.

Before he planted anything, he and Marcy sifted the dirt for stones. They each used a piece of screen that Mr. Endicott had nailed to four pieces of wood to make a tray. Squatting down with the spring sun on their backs, they sifted through the whole garden. Marcy whistled through her teeth. It was a habit she had picked up from Mr. Endicott.

One day her mother said, "Marcy, I have invited a friend to join us for dinner on Sunday."

"Who?" Marcy asked.

"His name is Mr. William Compton."

Something queer in her mother's voice made Marcy look at her sharply. Almost as quickly, her mother turned her head away, but not before Marcy could see she was blushing.

On Sunday afternoon at five o'clock Marcy put

on her white tights and her best white petticoat and her black patent leather shoes and her dark blue flowered cotton. When her mother came home from the office, she brought Mr. William Compton with her. Marcy looked at him with interest and curiosity.

"Marcy, this is Mr. Compton," her mother said.

Marcy arose from the sofa and said, "How do you do?" exactly as her mother had told her. Then all three of them went to Carswell's, and that night her mother had a little bit of sherry and Mr. Compton had a drink, but not beer, and Marcy had a Shirley Temple.

Mr. Compton asked her what grade she was in and what her teacher's name was and if she liked school. Mr. and Mrs. Carswell didn't come over to their table as they usually did, but they smiled at her and her mother and Mr. Compton from across the room. All the waitresses were smiling a lot, too. Her mother smiled the most, however, even when there wasn't anything to smile at except Mr. Compton. Marcy guessed what was going to happen. She guessed her mother was going to get married to Mr. Compton.

The next day Diane Walton said, "I saw you

and your mother and father at Carswell's last night."

"That wasn't my father," Marcy said sharply. "That was Mr. Compton. My father's name is Mr. Endicott."

Diane Walton was the brightest girl in the room. "Mr. Endicott!" she said. "Then how come your name is Benson?"

"Because," Marcy answered. She knew it wasn't a good answer so she walked away.

When she got home, she quickly changed her clothes and ran over to the Endicotts' screen door and pulled it, but the latch was on. Frowning, she looked up at the house. All the shades were drawn. Her heart began to thump heavily. Running around to the front of the house, she looked at the Endicotts' car. She even looked inside it to make sure it really was the Endicotts' car. It was. There in the seat was the mesh cushion Mr. Endicott liked to sit on because it let the air flow through. There, also, were Mrs. Endicott's sunglasses.

Turning, she stared at the house. All the front shades were pulled down, too. Suddenly she thought of the garden and ran around the side of the house and down the backyard. Reaching it, she felt like a hundred birds' wings were beating in her chest. All Mr. Endicott's tools were there, just thrown down on the ground. Mr. Endicott never left his tools like that. He had too much respect. A little moan escaped her lips, and she ran back to the Endicotts' door and pulled on it.

"Mr. Endicott?" she cried, and her voice didn't sound like herself. She began to shake all over. Something awful was the matter. Knowing this, she ran half stumbling back to her house to phone her mother. With shaking hands, she lifted the receiver and dialed.

"Barton Realty," a crisp voice answered.

"This is Marcy Benson. Is my mother there?"

"Who?" the voice said. And then, "Oh, Benson! Yes."

When her mother got on the line, her voice seemed astonishingly calm. "Hi, Marcy," she said.

"Oh, Mom, something awful's happened."

Instantly her mother sounded scared. "Marcy, what?"

"Over at the Endicotts'. The car is out front and the shades are all pulled down and the back door is latched."

"And what has happened?" Her mother didn't sound so scared now. She sounded cross.

Marcy began to cry. "I don't know but something has. All Mr. Endicott's tools are just lying in the garden."

"Marcy...!" her mother said sharply. "Now, Marcy, I want you to calm down and tell me exactly what the trouble is."

"Something has happened at Endicotts'."

"But what?"

Suddenly the full rush of tears burst. "I don't know! I want you to come home."

"But, Marcy..." There was a pause, and then her mother said very slowly, "The Endicotts' car is out front and the shades are down and the back door is latched. Is that it?"

With a supreme effort, Marcy added, "And Mr. Endicott's tools are lying in the garden."

"Well, Marcy, they've simply gone out for a walk or are taking naps or something like that."

Listening to her mother, Marcy began to believe this might be true.

"Marcy..." her mother said. "Marcy, are you there?"

"Yes."

"Did you have your cupcake?"

"Yes."

"All right, dear. Are you all right, now? I'll be home in a little while. All right?"

"Yes," Marcy answered and hung up.

She went out the door and crossed the yard to the Endicotts'. She felt foolish now. Her mother was probably right. The Endicotts had just gone off somewhere. She'd try the screen door once more. It might just have stuck. If it were only stuck and not latched, it meant that the Endicotts had gone out the back door. Grasping the handle, she tugged hard three times, and then her heart leaped up. There were footsteps from inside.

"Mr. Endicott?" she cried. "Mr. Endicott!"

She heard a bolt being worked unsteadily. Then she heard it being slid aside, and the door slowly opened.

"Hi, Marcy," Mr. Endicott said. His voice was blurry.

She stared at him. He didn't even look like Mr. Endicott. She knew he had been drinking. She could smell liquor, and he swayed back and forth, holding onto the door.

"Hi, Mr. Endicott," she said uncertainly.

For a long time he simply looked down at her, so Marcy said, "How is Mrs. Endicott?"

"Mrs. Endicott?" He waited a long time, then he said, "She's dead. She's dead! She's dead!

She's dead!" Then he slammed the door, and Marcy felt his sob slice through her.

She went down and sat in the swing under the pear tree. She was still sitting there when her mother came down across the yard to her. Her mother said, "I've just come back from Endicotts'. The family is all in there. Mrs. Endicott had a heart attack this morning. She's dead."

"I knew something had happened," Marcy said.

"Yes. You were right. I should have believed you. I'm really sorry, Marcy."

"That's O.K. Mrs. Endicott was dead by then."

"Yes." Her mother hesitated. "Come along in. It's time for supper."

"I have to do something first."

"What?"

"I have to pick up Mr. Endicott's tools in the garden."

"Could I help you?"

"No thanks."

She knew she had hurt her mother, but she didn't care. She crossed over to the Endicotts' garage and got the old Turkish towel that Mr. Endicott used for cleaning his tools. Then she went into the garden and wiped off the hand cultivator and the spade. The shovel wasn't a bit dirty. Mr. Endicott hadn't got around to using that when the heart attack happened. She gathered up these things and carried them back to the garage and hung them up where she knew they should go.

Chapter 11

For about a week there were a lot of people around the Endicotts': Mrs. Endicott's sister, who looked like Mrs. Endicott and even sounded like her when she talked, and the Endicotts' two grown sons and their wives. All the lights were always on at night, and Marcy was astounded to hear laughter. And then one afternoon she came home from school and the Endicotts' car was the only car parked out front and the shades were all drawn down, and she knew Mr. Endicott was alone again.

She didn't know what to do about it. Taking the dish of lime Jello her mother had left for her on the treat shelf, she ate it looking thoughtfully over at the Endicott house. Then she put the dish in the sink and ran a little water in it and went across the yard and tried the Endicotts' screen door. It was locked. She didn't knock or call. She knew Mr. Endicott didn't want to see her.

"Everyone takes grief a different way, dear," her mother said. "Mr. Endicott just wants to be alone now. In a while it will get easier."

Marcy looked at her mother, and her eyes filled with tears. "He'll die. He'll die of a broken heart."

Her mother sighed. "That rarely happens even when you want it to. Tomorrow I want you to go over to play with Wendy after school."

"I can't!" Marcy cried.

"Why on earth not?"

"I've got to be here. Just in case . . ."

"In case what?"

"In case Mr. Endicott comes out and wants to garden."

"Marcy . . ." her mother began firmly.

Marcy clapped both hands to her ears. "I can't!

I can't!" She squeezed her eyes tight and opened them. She did it several times. Then she and her mother stared at one another. They had both just realized she hadn't done that in a long time.

In her bed that night, Marcy could hear Mr. Compton and her mother talking downstairs. Mr. Compton came over almost every night now.

"You shouldn't indulge it, Janet," Mr. Compton was saying. "It's wrong. You've let her build up a dream world."

"Bill, he filled a very real need."

"Janet, believe me, I'll do my best to fill that need now. I like Marcy. She's a sweet little kid, and I intend to make a few things up to her. But you should have made her go to Wendy's."

It interested Marcy that Mr. Compton liked her, but her mother's voice sounded tired when she said, "It's not all that easy, Bill . . ." Pretty soon her mother would give in to Mr. Compton. Marcy knew that much.

The next day she decided she'd better go to Wendy's. Anyway, it was raining. At Wendy's house, Aunt Peg suggested that the girls make drawings.

"I'd rather write a composition," Marcy said. So she wrote a composition and Wendy made drawings. She entitled her composition:

81

THE GARDEN
by
Marcia Benson

My father and I planted a garden. We planted marigolds, zinnias, snapdragons, bachelor buttons. We planted tomato plants and raspberry bushes. Now they are growing under the ground. Someday I and my father will pick them. The End. P.S. All these words are perfectly spelled.

She knew they were perfectly spelled because Aunt Peg had spelled them. She could tell Aunt Peg was getting tired being interrupted to spell words, so Marcy was relieved when the composition was at last finished.

"May I read it, Marcy?" Aunt Peg said.

"No," Marcy answered. "It's a private matter."

When she got home, she went over to the Endicotts' back door and tried it, but she didn't really expect it to be open and it wasn't. Then she slipped the composition under the crack of the door so that a good inch of paper showed outside. The next morning before she went to school she went over to the Endicotts' and looked at the crack. There was no white paper showing, so she knew Mr. Endicott had found her composition, and when she got home from school, she saw immediately that the shades in the Endicott house were up. She tried the back door and it was open.

Her heart beat so hard that she could scarcely breathe. She walked through the pantry, which had a funny stale smell, and then she walked into the kitchen. Mr. Endicott sat at the kitchen table. He had her composition spread before him. Marcy was shocked because he looked so white and thin. His shirt collar stood out loose all around his neck. "Hi, Mr. Endicott," she said.

"Hi, Marcy. I read your composition. It's very good."

"I didn't do it at school, so I don't have to show it to my mom. You can just keep it."

"Thank you."

For a long time she just stood there and squeezed her eyes shut and open a couple of times, but she didn't let herself turn around and go home. Finally something came to her to say.

"Could I have a glass of water, Mr. Endicott?"

"What?" he said, and then he remembered his manners. "Oh, yes. Sure, sure." And he got up and got a glass from the cupboard and filled it with water and handed it to her. "You want some cookies, too?"

Marcy didn't but she said, "Yes, please," and Mr. Endicott opened the cupboard and took out a box of cookies. It was the same half-full box Mrs. Endicott had given her cookies from, and Marcy had to clamp her teeth tight to hold back tears.

"'Fraid these are stale," Mr. Endicott said.

"That's O.K." They were dry as dust, but Marcy forced herself to chew them up. Then she decided to take a chance. "Can we walk down to the garden?"

"If you want."

She was surprised that Mr. Endicott agreed. Walking down the backyard to the garden, she took another chance and slipped her hand into his. She was shocked that it was so lifeless, but she kept hanging on to it. At the garden, however, she let go.

"Mr. Endicott! Mr. Endicott! Look at it!"

All over the garden tender green tips showed above the ground.

"A lot of those are weeds," Mr. Endicott said.

"Shall we pull them out?"

"Better not yet, Marcy. Better wait so we can be sure which is a weed and which is a flower."

It was the first time Mr. Endicott sounded like himself again. Marcy thought she would explode.

That night Marcy's mother came into her room

and sat on the edge of her bed. She hadn't done that since Marcy was little except when she was sick, so Marcy knew something was coming.

"Marcy, you know I've been seeing a great deal of Mr. Compton. We're going to be married next fall."

"Oh," Marcy said, and then suddenly she thought of something and sat bolt upright. "Will we be moving away?"

"Yes, we'll be moving into a nice home over in Linden. All brand new."

Marcy's chin quivered. She pressed her lips together, and tears filled her eyes. The possibility of moving had never, never occurred to her. "Mr. Endicott . . ." she began and could go no further.

Marcy's mother took her hand. Marcy didn't like her mother holding her hand. It was too soft. But she forgot about that because her mother had said, "Mr. Endicott is moving away, too."

"He's not!"

"Yes, Marcy, he is. He called me this morning and asked me to put his house on the market. He wants to go back to his old town where he has friends."

Marcy's mouth dropped open. She felt a churning in her stomach as though there were big lumps down inside it rolling around trying to get out; as though there were screams down there.

"Marcy dear . . ." her mother began.

Finally the scream got out. "Go away!"

She cried herself to sleep. Her head under the covers, she cried while her mother said, "There, there, Marcy," and while Mr. Compton walked into the room and put his hand on her shoulder and said, "Now, now, Marcy, it can't be all that bad. Just wait till you see the fun we're all going to have in Linden." She hated her mother and Mr. Compton, but most of all she hated Mr. Endicott because he should have known she was better than friends.

The next day was a beautiful May Saturday, but Marcy didn't go over to the Endicotts'. She didn't even look over at the purple martin house as she always did ever since two purple martins had moved in there. She went down into her own backyard and sat on the swing. Presently she saw Mr. Endicott. He wore his gardening clothes. He crossed over to her yard and went up and knocked on the back door. He knocked a long time. Marcy let him. She didn't say a word.

He turned around and was going back to his yard when he saw her. "Oh, there you are," he said and came over to her. Marcy felt hot and sweaty. She started to swing, not looking at him.

"Hi, Marcy," he said. "I'm going to work in the garden. Want to help?"

She didn't answer. Mr. Endicott caught the rope and stopped the swing.

"Want to help in the garden, Marcy?"

"No."

He waited a bit, and then he said, "Your mom called me this morning. She said she told you that I'm moving away." He waited again. "I have to, Marcy. I can't stand the house anymore without Libby."

You still had me, she wanted to say, but she didn't. She had too much respect.

Then Mr. Endicott tried to turn things around. "You're going away, too, I hear."

Her head shot up. "I wouldn't have!"

"You would have to go with your mom."

"I wouldn't have! I'd have stayed!" She knew she was being foolish, but she didn't care.

Mr. Endicott sighed. "O.K., Marcy. Come help me with the garden. No point letting the flowers get choked out just because things go the wrong way."

She slid off the swing and walked beside him down to the garden, but she didn't take his hand.

One week later Mr. Endicott moved away.

Chapter 12

The new people wouldn't move in for a while, her mother told her, so after school Marcy worked in the garden every day. There was no point letting the flowers get choked out. Every now and then she would look around and expect to see Mr. Endicott cultivating the tomato plants or getting the hose set for *fine spray*. Sometimes she forgot and looked up to speak to him. And once she actually heard him call her name, and right out loud she said, "What did you say?" She wished she could tell Mr. Endicott that now she understood why he had to move away. Then she thought of writing a composition that she would send to him after she got the garden gear cleaned up.

She picked up the old towel she kept handy and wiped the dark, damp earth off her cultivator and dumped the basket of weeds and stuff on the compost heap. For a moment, she stood with her hands on her hips and surveyed the work she had accomplished that day. You could really notice any little improvement you made in a garden.

She wondered if the new people would keep it up. Maybe they wouldn't. It made her mad just thinking about that. Then she lifted her chin and looked at the purple martin house. Maybe the new people wouldn't give a hoot about a garden, but there was one thing that wouldn't change. Mr. and Mrs. Purple Martin would be coming back each springtime, still doing business at the same old stand.

When she got back to her house, she washed her hands and got out her notebook and pencil and sat up at the kitchen counter. She wrote:

GOING AWAY
by
Marcia Benson

My father had to move away because Mrs. Endicott died and he still saw her everywhere in the house, in the garden, on the stairs. Now I see my father everywhere, so I know what it is like. It is like that even flowers make you sad. And even birds singing and things like that. It is so awful because it hurts so hard and you can't bear it. It is better to go away. Soon I am going away with my mother and Mr. William Compton. The End.

She thought a moment and then added:

P.S. This was not written for school. It is a private matter.